TAUGHT BY A SWINGER

K.F. JONES

IT WAS late September when Alice arrived at the alternative fresher's fair. It was being held at an independent pub in the city centre, which regularly hosted niche events like local craft fairs, comic and art sales and gaming nights.

Alice had already attended the official freshers fair organised by the university's students union and signed up to all the usual things, earlier in the week. The whole week had been hectic. She'd met so many new people, and of course, the city was unfamiliar as well.

Cardiff was a maze of Victorian arcades and alleyways full of little shops and even boasted the oldest record shop in the world, although Alice wasn't quite sure why vinyl remained 'a thing'. There were shops selling skateboards, beads, vintage clothing, leather and she had noted with interest, a couple selling adult goods.

The Alt Freshers Fair was, however, a strictly unofficial event. There were some societies from the various universities represented here as well, but this wasn't supported by the student unions. Now that Alice was free of the constraints of her home life she was keen to meet new people, and have new experiences.

This was the event she'd been looking forward to since the summer when she'd first discovered that it would be the second year it was run. It was where the less mainstream societies were coming together to recruit new members. The more liberal societies such as the LGBTQ+ society were supportive and had a presence for anyone they'd missed at the main fair, but the Alt fair was really about those groups who were too small or didn't fit in with the general student union hierarchy.

Alice had been so excited at what today held for her that she had stopped off in the enormous and rather fancy shopping centre, ostensibly to go to the toilet. Technically she had been but immediately after she was done she had put her fingers to good use. She was working against the clock because she wanted to be on time so there was little teasing about it.

It felt so naughty to be frantically masturbating in the toilet of a shopping mall, and Alice tipped her head back, biting her lip as she listened to one of her favourite bands sexiest songs. She imagined she was being very discreet, but with her wireless earbuds in, she couldn't really tell how much noise she was making as her fingers slipped inside her wet pussy and her thumb teased her aching clit.

Alice had been impressed with the clean and spacious toilets, so much nicer than most shops had, probably just because the building wasn't all that old. As she imagined the tongue of a complete stranger working at her pussy, she idly fantasised about what this would be like in a tatty toilet in a rock club. The music banging away in the background and a ripped young man with tattoos on his knees, despite the peeling varnish and grime.

He would hungrily devour her pussy, teasing her lips and running his tongue up and down her wetness before sucking on her clit. When she came, his face would be covered in her juices, and he would unashamedly stand up, drawing her into a passionate kiss.

That would be when Alice knew that he was her plaything, available to her whenever she wanted. He was so needy, so submissive, that she'd be able to call on his services and not have to give back if she didn't want to. Alice wouldn't need to take his thick cock in her mouth and suck on him until he grunted and filled her mouth with his cum. But Alice did want that, and she imagined it in some detail.

Of course, in her fantasy it was much better than it had been in real life, mostly because she was actively enjoying it, relishing the flavour of him and his excitement at her touch. She would swallow his cum in a display like she'd seen pornstars do and he would look at her with adoration in her eyes.

Her orgasm was hurried but explosive, and her legs quivered as it ripped through her. Alice was about to reach for some paper to clean up, but then her eyes opened, and before she became fully aware of her surroundings she saw her glistening fingers.

She was reminded of the promise that she'd made to herself about becoming a different person. The person she wanted to be. A bolder, more exciting, more sociable version of her former self. This wasn't the Old Alice, this was the New Alice. The precocious Alice. The Alice who would be a new person at university. The Alice who was on her way to the daring alternative freshers fair. This Alice didn't merely wipe her hands when she'd cum.

After a moment's hesitation, she opened her mouth and put her wet fingers inside, sucking them clean, and savouring the taste of her own pussy. Alice had never done anything quite so naughty as masturbate in a public toilet before and she'd certainly never tasted herself. The taste was unusual but not as gross as her friends had said it would be to eat another girl out when they were giggling teenagers.

New Alice made sure to lick her fingers clean and beamed happily to herself when she was done. She wished she had someone to tell about how naughty she had been and hoped she'd make some new friends, more mature than her school friends, who would be far too shocked to discuss real sex.

Alice had moved beyond them. She was nineteen now, having taken a year out before university to grieve after her parent's tragic car accident. It was mostly just her now, and she'd already begun applying for jobs to help ease the financial pressure while she studied for her degree. Alice felt much more mature than her old friends, and she was the only one who'd come to Cardiff. That was a pity in some ways, but it also meant she felt liberated and free to build a new life.

She had cleaned up properly after her toilet adventure and then walked over to the pub, which was not far away. Cardiff's city centre was reasonably compact and could be crossed in about fifteen minutes at a brisk walking pace. There were cycles all over the place to be hired as well, and she resolved to look into that.

She wasn't sure she wanted to ride regularly enough to buy her own bicycle because she was used to being out on her mountain bike in the hills of the South Downs. Cardiff, on the other hand, was as flat as a pancake so the ride wouldn't be as exciting and New Alice was all about exciting rides. Alice giggled to herself at her naughty innuendo.

There was a charity who had been at the fresher's fair that repaired old bikes and sold them at cost. The manager had said they sometimes had part-time work going so she'd filled in an application for that, fixing her bike was second nature to Alice so it would be an excellent fit.

Plus there might be dishy cyclists about with muscular thighs and a fondness for tight shorts. Cycling had been perfect for Alice, she was a self-identified geek, and team sports never held much appeal. Her roleplaying group had always been cycling to one person's house or another, and she'd joined the university roleplaying society a couple of days ago.

Her heart was pounding in her chest, and she had to discreetly wipe her hands on her denim shorts. She didn't want clammy hands if anyone went for a handshake.

Alice stepped through the doorway of Mephistopheles and completed her metamorphosis into New Alice

THE VENUE WASN'T busy yet, Alice noted. She had timed her arrival well, it seemed. She strode confidently to the bar and ordered a half of a dark fruit cider that she'd discovered she liked. The woman behind the bar barely even glanced at her before asking for ID. Alice could feel the telltale heat of a blush rising as she fished for her purse which contained her brand new student union ID card.

While she fished that out, the woman began to pour the drink anyway. That gave Alice a little thrill. New Alice must look the part enough that she was just being checked as a guarantee, not because she still looked underage. Score one for her new clothes. The barwoman's eyes flickered up and down, and Alice felt a shiver up and down her spine. Was she checking her out? She was only young herself, Alice guessed, probably in her mid 20's. She produced her ID, and the woman squinted at it, "Nineteen already? Gap year?" she asked conversationally. "Two pounds, please. Special offer today for students."

"Yes, I had to take a year out," Alice said as she swiped her contactless card over the reader. The woman set a glass of dark purple liquid down in front of her. It looked more like blackcurrant squash than proper cider, but it was delicious and New Alice did not get shamed into drinking grown-up booze in massive quantities. Probably.

"Nice t-shirt. It suits you," the barwoman said. "I'm Natalie by the way." *That made sense thought Alice.* Natalie had been trying to read her t-shirt, which was as suggestive as she could bear to wear. It read, "You've been a naughty boy, come to my room."

Natalie leaned forward over the bar, revealing a generous cleavage, and flicked her head toward the stairs, "I think you want to be upstairs lovely, not down here."

Alice took a moment to look around her, and realised the societies on the ground floor were the tamer stuff at the alt fair, the rock music and LGBTQ+ society had tiny tables. It wasn't the biggest bar but it the decor screamed 'alternative', as did the devilish name. They'd probably put the tamer societies down here where the public could see them.

"Thanks, Natalie," Alice said, hoping the smile she flashed came across as more flirtatious and friendly than awkward and embarrassed. She made a beeline for the stairs to avoid anything getting weird.

Upstairs she found a handy sign, listing which groups were on this floor and the next. She spent a moment to absorb it all, checking off which ones she wanted to visit. There were already quite a few people up here, who must have been queued up to come in or hanging around the nearby shops and bars.

Alice checked her fitness tracker, it was already a quarter past ten in the morning. She resolved to visit the live roleplaying, roleplaying and boardgame societies last. She didn't really need to have a long or difficult conversation with them to know she wanted to join, it was a given.

The anime and manga society was a bit different because she'd always wanted to read and watch it but never knew where to start. She had already joined the LGBTQ+ society though mostly for solidarity not because she had been involved with women before, just entertained some fantasies. Alice thought of herself as a little curious but wasn't sure yet if New Alice would be brave enough to act on it.

It was on the top floor that her morning really took off. It was like stepping into another world. The first table was taken up with a display of all sorts of naughty things. There were blindfolds and Venetian masques, paddles, floggers and a bewildering array of sex toys. A local firm was sponsoring the event and was selling their wares here. It was like a beginners guide to vibrators, bondage and fetish wear. A cheerful middle-aged woman was staffing the stall and caught her eye.

Alice felt as if she'd been mesmerised, unable to break eye contact. "Come and have a look," the woman said in sultry tones. *Actual sultry tones thought Alice.* She had a voice like hot chocolate, delicious, inviting and creamy. Not in a million years would Alice ever have thought she would meet someone who genuinely had a sultry voice.

She smiled nervously and moved to the front of the table to pretend to look at the wares on offer. Alice certainly didn't mean to buy anything, even New Alice was blushing on the inside though she graciously prevented that from rushing to the surface.

"Gosh, this is all very interesting. What's the most popular thing?" Alice said, cringing inside even as she spoke the words. Why did the British insist on small talk? It would have been unpardonable to rudely turn away without at least saying something. She wished New Alice were already a lot braver than she felt.

"Oh, that's a good question. It's usually vibrators like this one. But then there are all sorts of goodies, handcuffs, candles for wax play because you need the right kind. Cock rings. Riding crops are very popular. Rope as well," the woman said, pointing things out as she went. "I'm Francesca by the way."

"Riding crops?" Alice asked as she shook Francesca's hand. The woman was gorgeous, probably in her mid-thirties and heavily made up. She had bottle-blonde hair and a smart business suit on, but one that showed off her impressive curves nicely and a colourful blouse to go with it, that was supported by a corset.

"Yes, they're very visually appealing, people find," the woman replied. "Can I show you anything?"

"Um. I'm not sure."

"We have this Freshers Bag. There's a vibrator, a butt plug, a little paddle, some leatherette cuffs, lube and some condoms. All yours for ten pounds. It's great for people just starting their collection," the stallholder said.

Alice chewed her lip, but it didn't take more than a couple of seconds for her to buy a little bright red gift bag full of delights. They weren't anything special but enough to have some fun with and try some things out for a very reasonable price.

Before she came up to Cardiff to settle in, Alice had looked around for toys she might buy but had decided to hold off until she was in the city, so she was familiar with the prices and which toys looked high quality. These ones were cheap and cheerful but would be fine for a bit of experimenting.

Alice thanked the stallholder who gave her a few leaflets and explained their shop was in Roath, where most of the places students rented were found. "We offer all the usual student discounts, of course. Have you been to an adult shop before?"

"No, not yet, I haven't dared," Alice said.

"I understand that. First-time jitters are to be expected, we get a lot of people who walk by several times in one day before finally coming in. But you needn't worry. Come along to the shop, and I'll give you a guided tour, I do love to flaunt my wares for newbies," Francesca said.

"You wouldn't mind? I think I might have a lot of questions," Alice said.

"Goodness no. It's my shop, and I'm proud of our customer service. I like to say, everyone who asks for help, leaves completely satisfied."

"I'll think about it," Alice said, making to leave but the woman held her hand up and walked around the table.

"I don't do this for everyone, but you seem a bit nervous, so I want to make sure your first experience is a good one. Are you free tomorrow by any chance?"

"Yes, I am as it happens, I don't have any set plans yet."

"The shop doesn't normally open until 1 pm on Thursdays because I'm a bit short-staffed at the moment. If you can make it by say ten am, I'll open up early for you and just for you. Then I can give you a private tour of the place. How does that sound? Would it help?"

"Thank you so much, that would be lovely, Francesca. I'll be there at ten, or would earlier be better?"

"Nine thirty would be even better, then you can have as much time browsing as you want and if you don't need me to help, I can do some paperwork. I think you'll find it fascinating, we have lots of toys, lingerie, bondage gear and all sorts. Whatever you need, Alice, I can provide it, and I absolutely love showing customers how things work. You'll have a wonderful time, I promise, and I insist that you ask any questions you want. I've heard it all, and I promise I won't laugh or poke fun. I'm an excellent teacher, if I do say so myself," Francesca said with a warm smile.

"Honestly, it sounds absolutely wonderful. I can't wait."

"Me neither, I'm usually all 'work, work, work'. It'll be great to just have some good old fashioned fun in the shop for a change. See you tomorrow, you best get on with joining your groups, or you'll be here all day."

Alice looked at the business card, which had a tiny map printed on the reverse. It was in the same neighbourhood as her little studio flat, so it wasn't going to be hard to pay it a visit. It was nothing special, but she had privacy, and it wasn't too much of a strain on the small amount of money her parents had left her. She knew she'd have to resist the temptation to visit the shop and buy lots of expensive toys.

It was time for her next stop. Deeper into the room was a table staffed by a few people. Their homemade posters proclaimed them to be Kink Soc. All their volunteers were already talking to interested students, so she nonchalantly walked past them as if they hadn't been her main target.

Alice chatted for a few minutes with a nice lady from the Erotica & Romance Society and signed up to their mailing list. She was studying physics, but her love of roleplaying had her deeply involved in how stories were planned, so perhaps she'd try her hand at some writing one day?

She stood off to the side, pretending to read the writers leaflet, but keeping an eye on the KinkSoc table so she could approach them when they were free to talk. Alice shuffled her feet, moving about as she tried to make it look like she was deeply absorbed, nodding as if she was approving of what she read.

"I think they're going to be a while," someone said behind her.

Alice turned around to see who had spoken. "They're very popular, and people have a lot of very earnest conversations with them at great length."

"I'm sorry?"

"KinkSoc. That was who you were lingering about to speak to, right?" the tall young woman asked. Her black hair fell to her shoulders and, despite her height, her figure was curvy in all the right places, not model thin. She had tanned complexion that gave her a Mediterranean appearance.

The stand behind them featured a heraldic device consisting of a large sock, over which a pendulum was clearly in motion. Puzzling.

"Um. Yes. I don't want to interrupt them," Alice said.

"Gotcha. Why don't you talk to Freya and I instead? I'm Olivia," the tall young woman said, gesturing toward the redhead next to her who was about the same height as Alice, around 5'7".

"Okay. I'm Alice, pleased to meet you."

"Hi!" the redhead said. "I'm Freyja."

Olivia rolled her eyes. "Yes, I already said that."

"I know, but people never understand it the first time, I always have to tell them at least twice before they remember it," Freyja retorted.

"So, um, what society is this?"

"I told you we should have put the name on the heraldry," Freyja said. She looked at Alice, "No-one ever gets it without being told. I think we'll have to change it."

"Pendulum sock? Sock pendulum?" Alice tried, sounding them out but she definitely hadn't got it right.

"Told you," Freyja said, playfully punching Olivia on the arm.

"Stop it, or I'll give you such a spanking," Olivia said.

Freyja stuck her tongue out. "Not bloody likely, not my scene darling."

Olivia sighed. "See what I have to deal with? She's not really that kinky, so you can't punish her," she said with a shrug and a grin that said she wasn't really annoyed.

"I think you're going to have to spell it out I'm afraid, though I think I'm going to kick myself," Alice said, her interest in the society for BDSM aficionados forgotten for the time being.

"So this is a pendulum, and what do they do?"

"They oscillate about the equilibrium position?" Alicia ventured.

"Physics?" Olivia groaned.

Alice nodded. Olivia waved her hand in a circle, motioning for Alice to go on. She pondered for a second, "They swing?". Olivia beamed at her and clapped her hands. Progress. "Swing. Sock. SwingSoc?"

"Yes, got it in several. We are the founding members of SwingSoc, Cardiff's newest society for students, of all universities," Olivia said proudly.

"It's an exercise thing, then? You got to the parks and play on the swings?"

Freyja just about wet herself laughing. Olivia glared at her, "See, that's why I didn't want to put a swing set on the poster."

She turned back to Alice and with a thin smile, as she tried desperately to ignore her friend's hysterics, "No, Alice. SwingSoc is for students who want to get involved in the local swinging scene. We organise socials, give advice and mentoring, run a forum and introduce people to the non-student scene."

Swingers? A student society for swingers? Well, it was no more unusual than KinkSoc, but she hadn't heard of them before she came to the fair.

"Would you like to join up?" Olivia asked, holding out a clipboard and pen.

3

ALICE TOLD herself that she had filled out Olivia's paperwork and paid the nominal joining fee because of the awkward peer pressure of the moment. That was the story in her mind when she imagined anyone asking her, at least.

In reality, a brief further conversation with Olivia about the society had left her netherlips dripping with arousal. Freyja chiming in hadn't helped, the vivacious redhead was sex on legs, and Alice was pretty sure she could have sold anything she cared to.

After the Alternative Fresher's Fair finished, there was to be a break to tidy stuff away, and then Olivia and Freyja were running a social evening for any new SwingSoc members. Olivia had invited her, explaining it was just like a BDSM munch. There would be conversations with like-minded people, in a pub that served drinks and food and no play of any kind, nor nudity.

Alice had been happy to agree to come along. KinkSoc didn't have anything going on tonight according to their poster, and Olivia explained their committees tried to avoid clashes over timetables where possible. That meant it wouldn't disrupt Alice's primary goal of connecting with KinkSoc today or prevent her from attending whatever their first event was.

When Olivia had her firm commitment, she gently guided Alice over to a nearby stand, where a young man and woman, clearly a couple, were waiting hopefully.

The stand behind them bore the legend, NaturSoc and the sub-title, Cardiff Student Naturist Society, est. 1997.

"Carol, Bob, this is Alice. She's new, and she'd love to hear all about your society, wouldn't you Alice?" Olivia asked. Alice nodded dumbly, too surprised to respond. First, she'd been invited to a party for swingers, and now she was being introduced to people who wanted to be naked all the time. Whatever next?

Politely, she shook their hands as Olivia left them to it. "Have you ever tried naturism?" Bob asked but to his credit, Alice felt, without the slightest hint of a leer.

She shook her head. "No. I've never had the um, opportunity," Alice ventured.

"That's ok. It's not nearly as big a deal as people think. People who grew up in clothing-optional environments have no problems with social nudity. It removes a lot of baggage from one perception of being naked on your own, not just in groups. Plus it's fun," Carol said.

"You're probably wondering where we do it, right? It's not all the beaches you know. We use Kenfig Burrows, which is a bit of a trek but we go out as a group and make a day of it. There are a few naturist camping sites and clubs around that we visit as well. We've been going for years, so the society has good links with the community," Bob said.

"What do you do then? Just get together and be naked?"

"More or less. There's usually a lot of outdoor sports like mini-ten, boules, tennis, swimming, that sort of thing. Plus sunbathing, reading, talking to people. The clubs have barbeques and bars and pool tables and table tennis and things. People play volleyball or other games at the beach," Carol clarified.

"It sounds like a lot of travelling and what about winter? Isn't it a bit cold!" Alice asked.

"Yes, we'll have a few visits if the weather is good, all jam-packed into September and if we're lucky October but after that, we use the clubs and have socials in houses. There are some meets at swimming pools, and saunas around that we can travel to fairly easy. That's the great thing about Cardiff. You can be in Swansea, Newport or Bristol in 45 minutes or less so we can get to lots of events really easily," Carol said.

"That's cool, so you have meetings at people's houses in Cardiff then?" Alice asked.

"Yup," said Bob, "Our second years try and arrange houses together. There are some houses in Cardiff that have six or ten student bedrooms. You can hold great house parties, and when someone gets a good one, we try and pass it on to the next year's students. There are a few private parties as well with, well, 'adult's but I mean people who are working and have big houses sometimes put on a private barbeque," Bob explained.

"And you can just be naked all the time? Don't the guys get a bit, excited?"

"Sometimes, but we just politely ignore it, and they go off some-where private until they can calm down. Some of the swimming pools can cool you off pretty quickly," Bob replied.

"And couples don't get a bit, you know…"

"Frisky?" Carol teased. "No, none of that I'm afraid. The clubs and beaches are family environments, so it's just people meeting up and relaxing in a place where they can be naked without fear and not feel they have to conform to prudish views. Of course, there are other parties for that sort of thing."

Bob nodded sagely, agreeing with his other half.

"We saw you talking to SwingSoc," Carol said cautiously. "Did you join up?"

"Yes," Alice replied, feeling bold. Somehow it didn't seem like either Carol or Bob were the sort of people to be prudish about anything, let alone swinging.

"Cool. I hope you enjoy it, they have a lot of fun I know, and they're mad keen to recruit open-minded people because they're brand new this year. It's hard to get a society going and keep it going," Carol said.

"Are you members? If it's not too rude to ask. I don't know what's polite and what's invasive yet."

Bob replied, "Nah. Our sexy times are a lot tamer than that. We're strictly vanilla."

Carol let out a delightfully dirty laugh at that statement, pushing him on the shoulder. "Oh you big fibber, Bob," she said as he struggled to keep upright.

"What?" he exclaimed, a little confused.

Carol turned back to Alice and leaned in to whisper conspiratorially, "Have you heard of CFNM? Or CMNF?"

"Oh that," Bob said, looking a little sheepish.

Alice stepped forward, right up to the edge of their trestle table of leaflets. "No, it doesn't ring a bell. Should it?"

"It stands for 'clothed female, nude male'. Or vice versa, or you can have clothed female, nude male," Carol explained, still whispering.

"Mmm. That sounds fun. Is it a naturist thing?"

"Strictly speaking, no but some people into naturism are a bit kinky or interested in swinging, you just don't cross over at our main events," Carol said.

"What's this got to do with Bob, though?" Alice said, rather enjoying how uncomfortable Bob was looking but playing along with Carol, who seemed not to care.

"Bob found out about it and persuaded me to go with him to a CFNM party for a bit of a lark," Carol said. "Me and a few other ladies, all dressed up to the nines in our little black dresses, and a group of men, all stack bollock naked. They had them going around, serving drinks, giving us foot massages, painting our toenails."

"That sounds amazing."

"It was. Great fun but the best bit wasn't the party. When we got home, we couldn't wait to get each other naked again. The sex was amazing all weekend," Carol confided, with a dreamy look on her face.

"Did you ever try it? You know, being naked while he's clothed," Alice asked.

"No. I looked into it, and those parties get a bit racy more often than not. The ladies end up on their knees giving blowjobs in front of everyone," Carol said.

"That didn't happen at the party you went to?"

"A couple of the guys did get their heads put under a skirt, but you didn't get to see anything," Bob said. "It's not the same thing, but some parties are more sexual than others as we understand it."

"Still, it sounds like you'll be doing it again to me," Alice giggled.

Carol and Bob both nodded enthusiastically. "When the hot weather is over, we'll have another look for a party I think," Carol said. "Bob wants me to go to a CFNF party too."

That was intriguing, Alice thought. "As the clothed one or the naked one?"

"Either or both, he's not fussed. He just wants to hear about what happens," Carol said.

"Naughty boy. Are you going to do it? Are you, you know, into girls?" Alice asked.

"I could, but I haven't done anything like it before, so I'm not just going to go and get naked for some women for Bob's jollies," Carol said.

"I sense that there is a reason you would," Alice said.

Carol nodded and giggled. "It'll never happen, but I said I'd do CFNF if he would do CMNM, as the nude obviously."

Bob shook his head. "Nope. Nope." Carol gave him a lascivious grin and pulled him in for a kiss.

"Awww. Is my sweetie afraid of the big penises? Who's a fraidy little naturist, hmm?" Carol said.

Bob grumbled something Alice didn't catch. "As you can see, Alice, he's still a work in progress, but he's not always so reticent. In private when he's excited, he's close to agreeing to it. He wants me to take pictures of the all-girl party if I go to one and he's so keen that he's not far from agreeing to the same for me," Carol bragged.

Bob laughed nervously. "Not true, not true at all. Wild exaggeration," he said, though his words sounded hollow. Alice had a mental flash of him on his knees, being guided toward an armchair by a leash that was attached to a collar around his neck. She could see why Carol was teasing him about that. It was certainly hot enough to be added to Alice's growing list of fantasies.

"Anyway, enough naughtiness. If you want to come to our next meet, we're planning for Sunday at our place. Mostly just a meet and greet for newbies because the weather is looking to be bad, but if it brightens up, we will change to a beach visit instead. My contact details are on the card, so just reach out if you need any questions answered or want to come along," Carol said.

Alice thanked them for the information about the naturist group and the fun chat, and then, seeing a couple of open spaces at the KinkSoc table, she made her excuses and left them to it.

She was feeling a lot more confident after speaking to Olivia, Freyja, Carol and Bob. Their openness had been a breath of fresh air, and Alice was energised by their honesty.

4

"Hi, I'm Tom, this is Jessica, and that's Kate," the rather dishy chap staffing the KinkSoc stand said. Jessica was a big curvy girl, in a beautiful summer dress with a black choker on, that was suggestive to Alice in context, but she wouldn't have thought twice about. Tom looked like a surfer or swimmer, with long curly blond hair and a tight, long-sleeved t-shirt that suggested serious muscles lay under it.

Kate was talking to a nervous-looking young man, who looked to Alice like a submissive waiting to happen. He could barely maintain eye contact with her, but she was so impressed with his resilience. He was sticking it out despite being a nervous wreck. Good for him. Over the summer, she'd tried to go to a local munch for the first time but couldn't make it through the doorway. Kate was slender and bespectacled, wearing all black, with studded leather wristbands, nose piercings and one side of her head shaved.

"Hi, I'm Alice. I wanted to join KinkSoc if I may?"

"Just like that? No questions?" Jessica asked.

"Maybe a few but you seem really busy, and I'm really sure I want to join," Alice said.

"Cool. We have a table back here to sign up at, we do everything we can online," Tom said, gesturing to a screened-off area behind them. "If you can go and sit with Jessica she'll get you sorted out and then I can talk to the next people. Feel free to ask any questions you have though, Jessica is way more knowledgeable than I am anyway so you're in good hands and you can always pop by later if you're sticking around the fair."

"Great thanks, Tom," Alice said, following Jessica behind the exhibition stands that were festooned with posters that explained what kink was, or what safe, sane and consensual meant. Alice had done so much research she was already familiar with the terminology and a whole range of kinks and fetishes.

"Pull up a seat," Jessica said, sitting down next to her, so they were both facing a laptop.

Alice sat down and immediately recognised the website open on the tab.

"So, what we have here is our website on one tab, where you can fill in some basic info, for now, then we have BDSMInformed. That's a free public site that most kinky people use, a community for us if you will," Jessica said. "You don't have to give us lots of details, for your own privacy but we need at least a name and an email address that you go by. It can be a new email if you want to separate it out and haven't thought to get a grown-up one before you came here. Some people turn up with all sorts of funny addresses, they've had since they were young! I'd like to encourage you to provide more information than less, that way the committee get to know you a bit better, and our chaperones can look after you more easily. You can update your profile later, of course, we just have to create a login today. If you join the other website, which we encourage you to do, that's not ours, but it's a great way to communicate with people on the scene who aren't students. Only people in our society are allowed on our own site, except for past members. They're allowed to stay, but you can filter them out."

"Ok, I understand," Alice said.

"Did you get all that? I know I tend to gabble. This isn't really my strength. Do you want me to repeat anything?"

"No, that's fine, I think I got it all," Alice said.

"I get the impression you know at least a little about the scene, by the way, you didn't want to ask questions, but there's no need to be embarrassed in the slightest. I will answer any question that's not about African vs European swallows, ok?"

Alice couldn't help smiling at that. Anyone who was a fan of the Holy Grail was alright by her. "Thanks, Jessica."

"You can call me Jess, that's fine, but I don't mind Jessica."

"Thanks then, Jess. I've already got a profile on the lifestyle site. Do you want to see it?"

"If you don't mind showing me, that's cool, but mostly I want to get you invited to our groups on there if you want to join. It makes it easier for you to keep track of events and things," Jess explained.

They went through the process of getting Alice's BDSMInformed profile invited to the KinkSoc groups, and Jess added her as a friend as well, after Alice confirmed she could. Then Alice filled in the necessary details for her login to the KinkSoc site which was very cleverly done. Jess explained they had several computer science students who'd worked on it over the last few years and it got better all the time.

"Are you dominant or submissive?" Jess asked, "If you don't mind me prying?"

"I'm not sure yet, I've never done anything like this," Alice said.

"That's cool. Don't let anyone push you around, you have any problems, you ask me or Tom or Kate, ok? Look, if you need a mentor to guide you in the lifestyle, just let me know. I'll help you find someone you like that can look after you, show you around events, explain types of play to you, whatever you need," Jess said.

"Really?"

"Yes, absolutely. We're a lovely community, and we look after people as much as we can. Don't let all the spanking, and cries of ecstatic pain and the scary clothes fool you. We're all about looking after each other. Whatever you need to learn, there's a mentor who can teach you, and you are bound to be popular," Jess said.

Alice assumed that meant she was good looking, which she'd been told before but always felt a little strange about when she was complimented. "Because these mentors want to find young women to shag?" Alice said.

"No, it's not like that. A mentor could be anyone with experience and often a bit older, but they could be dominant or submissive. They usually teach play skills like how to play with wax or rope bondage safely. You might decide you want to be tied up to feel what it's like, or spanked perhaps. But it's not about sex or romantic relationships. If that's what you want, we should find you someone else. Lots of people have their sexual partner for kink, but they still see a mentor who can teach them safely about types of play. A spanking is quite simple to do safely, but needles are a skill, and you should always know what you're doing before you play in a new way," Jess explained.

"So if I wanted to find out what spanking was like?" Alice pondered.

"Yeah, I could introduce you to a Domme woman or a Dom man who could spank you, just as a play scene. Then you could feel what it was like with someone trustworthy. You could do it at a club night or in private, whatever works for you. We have skills sessions for things like ropework too, where we teach each other and practice. There's no sex, but you can bet the couples go home and have sex afterwards in a lot of cases," Jess said with a wicked grin.

"Thanks. It sounds cool. It's good to know people will help you," Alice said.

"Don't ever hesitate to ask, ok? Have you got any more questions for now? There's a munch during the day on Saturday, if you're free. Here, I'll send you an invite," Jess said, looking up the society website on her phone. "It's in here actually. Lots of our alternative societies use Mephistopheles for their get-togethers."

"Brilliant, thanks so much, Jess. I don't have any more questions for now. Can I message you?"

"Day or not, pal! Yeah, ok, that sounded cheesy, I hear it. But seriously, message away, I might not answer if my phone is on mute or you know, I'm all tied up," Jess said with a big wink, getting a laugh from Alice. "But I'll get back to you as soon as I can. If Tom is the one who is tied up, of course, I'll be able to get back to you quicker."

"You're an item?" Alice blurted out. "I mean, is he your dom? I didn't realise."

"No, we're both switches. We swap being in charge, and there's no reason for you to have known we were together. We don't get all touchy-feely in public that much, I mean, outside of the club nights but that's different," Jess said.

"I hope he knows how lucky he is," Alice said.

"If he ever forgets, I have plenty of ways to remind him of his place," Jess said with a wink.

"I bet you do," replied Alice and they both fell about laughing until Tom stuck his head around the stand to find out what was going on. They clammed up quickly, and he returned to the table out front with a frown.

The two women watched him go then fell about laughing.

BEFORE SHE LEFT, Olivia convinced Alice to join the photography society, AltPhotoSoc. They were a group that mixed with lots of other groups, and they did everything from landscapes to erotic photography classes. Olivia had a hard time convincing Alice at first, until she whipped out her phone and showed some pictures of herself on her knees, with a thick cock in her mouth.

Olivia took delight in her blushing reaction but was clearly happy when Alice practically grabbed the phone of her and scrolled through a few more pictures. For her part, Alice found herself wet again, seeing Olivia fucking and sucking some guy, in front of a photographer no less. Apparently, this particular photographer was a woman as well, which somehow made it hotter to Alice.

Finally, she'd gone back downstairs and joined all the gaming societies who were there. She certainly wasn't going to be short of things to do for the next few years.

Now it was early evening, and she was back at Mephistopheles, to attend the SwingSoc social evening. Olivia had texted her to 'dress to impress' so she was wearing one of her favourite little black dresses which included a body contouring number with a plunging neckline and strappy back. It left just enough to the imagination to be titillating, and she hoped everyone would like it.

Olivia was waiting by the door for her, and practically pounced on her the moment she came in. "Fucking hell, Alice, I thought you were cute, but you scrub up really well, don't you?"

Before she could answer, Olivia had steered her over to the bar and ordered them cocktails. "Just a treat for you to celebrate your first time, I'm not buying drinks for you all night, far too expensive," Olivia said. Then she leaned in and whispered in Alice's ear, "Actually, I switch to soft drinks after just the one, so I don't get squiffy and do anyone I might regret."

Alice had to cough to avoid choking on her drink and Olivia wasn't sympathetic at all, having a good laugh at her expense while she spluttered. "Come on over here," Olivia said, pulling gently at her wrist, "I have something I want to talk about."

They sat down at a high table, shoulder to shoulder so they could hear each other over the background music, which wasn't too loud but didn't make conversation easier. "What are you into, Alice? I've not had a chance to ask."

"What do you mean?" Alice asked, dreading the answer but stalling for time.

Olivia rolled her eyes theatrically. "Come on, don't play silly buggers, you know. What do you like sexually? Will you tell me? You don't have to, but I'd like you to. I've got a good reason."

"Which is?"

"I want to find you, someone, to play with. Tonight. I want you to be one of our best members, the people who show others just how amazing our society is. I want you to love every minute of this social and your first time playing and if I can make that happen for you tonight, and you're ready, I figure you'll be a lifelong member of SwingSoc. Honest enough for you?" Olivia asked.

"You want me to play tonight? Here?" Alice almost shrieked.

Olivia reached out and placed a comforting hand on Alice's wrist, gently stroking her, as if she was trying to restore calm, "There there, it's not a big deal. You don't have to, Alice. This is just a social anyway, but I think you're really keen to spread your wings, aren't you? If I'm right, I promise I can help if you let me."

Alice took a deep breath and nodded. "I'm so nervous."

"Don't be, there's no need. Nothing is going to happen you aren't in control of, ok?"

Alice nodded. "Yeah."

"Cool. So, what's your deal then? Boys? Girls? Both? What gets you going?"

"Mmm. Boys definitely," Alice said.

"But girls, maybe, am I right?" Olivia said with a wink.

Alice blushed again. "Yes. Maybe, I'm not sure."

"Shall we put a pin in that question for now then, and stick with boys?"

"Yes, please. I hope you don't mind. You're not disappointed in me?" Alice asked.

"Dear me, no. You go at whatever pace works for you, honey. If you want to play with ladies, more power to you. I love it, but it doesn't mean you have to," Olivia said.

"Thanks. I'm just not sure I'm ready for... you know."

"Pussy licking?" Olivia said, laughing hysterically when Alice's hand involuntarily covered her mouth in shock.

"Yes, I'm definitely not ready for pussy licking, Olivia," Alice hissed.

"Oh, your face, it's a picture of innocence. Classic. Ok, what are you ready for then, beautiful lady?"

"How about cocksucking?" Alice bragged.

"How about it? It's fantastic! How about that guy over there? Does he meet with your approval? The one with the smart blazer and jeans combo?" Olivia asked.

"I could never pull him," protested Alice. Olivia ignored her, her thumbs typing furiously at her smartphone.

Alice went back to her drink but before she'd even had two more good sips of the fruity alcoholic beverage, the name of which she couldn't remember, jeans and jacket had sauntered over to their table and was stood next to Olivia.

"You rang?" he said, putting on a posh butler voice.

"Why yes I did, Alex. Meet Alice, Alex. She's a fresher and she'd dying to have some fun, aren't you Alice."

Alice almost choked on her drink but managed to glare at Olivia. "I'm not dying to. It's not that bad."

Olivia glanced around the bar to check no-one was really watching. "Alex," she said, reaching out and tugging him closer by his belt. "Can I give her a peek?" she asked. Alex nodded and casually sipped his drink as if nothing untoward was going on.

Olivia unbuckled his belt and pulled the top few buttons of his jeans apart. Alice tried to shrivel into a little ball but couldn't so her eyes remained transfixed on Alex's crotch. His fly was parted now, and his black boxers were clearly visible. Alice looked around, and no-one was even looking at them, not that they could have seen much from behind Alex's broad back and his jacket.

A moment later, Olivia casually reached her right hand down between the hem of Alex's shorts and his promisingly muscular waistline. Alice could see the bulge before she even withdrew it, and it was a struggle to remain calm. She couldn't quite believe Olivia was doing this in a bar, even one that was reserved for a private function and theoretically populated with only swingers. Regardless of Alice's doubts, Olivia fished his cock out and presented it for inspection.

For inspection by Alice. He wasn't hard, but he was clearly enjoying himself, Alice could see. It was a good looking, uncut cock. His pubic hair was neatly trimmed, which was appealing to her, and he was in good physical shape. Olivia looked at her, "Want to touch it?"

Alicia had reached out and tentatively stroked the cock before she'd even nodded her consent.

"Nice, isn't it? Not too much now, he won't be able to put it away," Olivia cautioned. Alice reluctantly withdrew her hand, wishing she could just shove it straight between her legs that minute.

Olivia expertly tidied Alex's cock away and did him up, asking quietly as she worked, "Do you want to suck it?"

"Yes. Yes, I do," Alice confirmed.

"Take him in the toilets then. Now." Olivia suggested. Alice hesitated for a moment, and Olivia urged her on, "Do it, Alice. Go to the toilet with him and suck that nice cock."

Alice swallowed, looking back and forth from Alex's crotch to Olivia a few times before she leaned over and whispered in Olivia's ear, "I'm nervous."

"What will make you less nervous, cutie?" Olivia asked.

"Would you come in and watch. You know, to make sure I'm safe," Alice asked.

Olivia smiled sympathetically. "Of course I will, Alice. Anything I can do to calm your nerves, you just let me know. Come on, we'll go first, and he can join us," Olivia said, standing up and whispering something in Alex's ear.

Alice stood up and followed Olivia to the toilets, down a little corridor at the back. Olivia pulled them into the disabled toilet and when Alice asked she pointed out there were no disabled people in the place, and she knew that for a fact because none had yet asked to join the society and it was a private night. Her objection countered, Olivia gently guided Alice to sit on the closed toilet seat.

Alex joined them a moment later and locked the door behind him. "Pleasure to meet you, Alice," he said.

"Nice to meet you too. Would you come closer, please?" Alex did as he was asked, and New Alice reached out, grabbing his belt and pulling him forward until his shins touched the bowl of the toilet, between her knees. Swiftly she unbuckled his trousers and pulled the button fly apart, letting the trousers drop to the floor in a puddle around his ankles.

Alice could see his cock was stiff beneath his jockey shorts. Before she could move, Olivia got behind him, gripped each side of his shorts in one hand, and dropped into a squat, dragging them smoothly down to join his trousers. She then stood by their side, so she had a good view.

Alice already had a good view. Alex's cock wasn't enormous, but it was a perfectly good size, she knew. It was already tumescent even before she took it in one hand and rolled the foreskin back down his shaft. She ran her tongue over the tip of his cock before old Alice could interfere with her progress.

A moment later, she had the hot, velvety head of his engorged cock in her mouth and was sucking hard, as she tried to work her tongue over it.

Olivia made appreciative noises, "Nicely done, Alice. Give me your phone." Her tone was insistent, and Alice had handed over her smartphone before she'd even considered what Olivia wanted it for.

By the time Olivia took the first picture, Alice was just realising what was going on, and here eyes were bulging as her mouth filled with thick cock. She pulled her head back and squeaked, "What are you doing?" at Olivia.

"I'm preserving it for history. Believe me, it's a thrill to have your first time on camera," Olivia said. "You'll cherish these pictures. Never let them use their phone, by the way, retain ownership at all times."

"It's not my first time sucking cock, Olivia," Alice hissed.

"Definitely not," Alex chimed in, going instantly quiet when Olivia glared at him.

"First time swinging, Alice. Please? We can delete them later if you don't like them. Alex won't mind, will you love?"

"No, I love it. Just don't put my face on any websites, deal?"

Alice sighed and remembered her vow to get New Alice off to a good start when she reached university.

Alex's head rolled back as the beautiful young woman's mouth enveloped his cockhead, and she began sucking at him hard, as her head bobbed up and down. Alice's hands stroked his shaft and Olivia was taking as many pictures as she could.

"I'm going to cum. This is amazing," warned Alex, breathing hard.

Alice looked up at him, her lips curling in a smile briefly and gave him a big thumbs up.

"I think that means go right ahead, Alex. My, my, my. What a find we have here," Olivia said as she dropped to her knees beside them and moved forward to get close-ups of the action. All the time, the camera was taking snaps of Alex's cock as it was covered with Alice's mouth and uncovered again.

When his thighs started to shake, and Alice had to hold him in place with one hand on his cock and one on his hips, it was obvious to Olivia that he was coming, and coming hard. Alice continued to work at him until his pulsing cock subsided, and she drew back.

Alice beamed at Olivia happily but didn't speak. The tall raven-haired girl held the phone up in one hand, selfie-style and took photos of Alice and her as she snuck in to plant a puckered kiss on Alice's lips. Alice motioned for her to do it again, clearly enjoying the photo session and they pressed their lips together a few times while Olivia took photos, and Alex muttered encouragement.

A strange look crossed Olivia's face, and Alice knew she'd tumbled something. "Hey, you haven't swallowed, have you?" Alice smiled back mischievously and shook her head.

"You filthy bitch!" Olivia said, not diminishing Alice's happiness one iota. "Go on then, show us, you know you want to."

Alice tipped her head back and slowly opened her mouth while Olivia took more pictures. Her tongue was covered in a pool of thick white cum. "Fuck me, that's so hot," Alex said.

"You're damned right it is. Alice, you are so sexy. I wish you liked girls so I could kiss you and share that lovely big load," Olivia said. Alice looked at her for a second, her mouth still wide open in the sluttiest display she could manage, inspired by countless hours of watching pornstars do this. After a moment, New Alice gave her new friend, Olivia a big thumbs up and Olivia squealed in delight.

The tall girl handed Alex the phone, and he began taking photos, while Olivia placed a hand on either side of Alice's face to guide her, then leaned in for a kiss. At first, she used her tongue to lick stray dribbles of Alex's cum from Alice's chin. Then she dipped her tongue into Alice's mouth, before finally locking them together in a hot, cummy kiss.

The two young women kissed passionately, sharing Alex's cum between them for a while before Olivia leaned back and they both swallowed. "Fuck me. Fuck me," Alex had muttered throughout as he watched the sexy display. Alice was amazed that she'd already snowballed let alone having kissed a girl to boot. When she'd done swallowing and licking Alex's cock and Olivias face clean of his cum, she smiled up at them happily.

"I told you I wasn't new at cocksucking," she said, happily.

"You certainly did," Olivia replied. "Here's the evidence to prove it," she said as he handed the phone back to Alice.

Alex gasped as Alice's hand wrapped around his cock and began to pump it back and forth. "Any chance you can go again, big boy?" Alice asked.

"Yeah, but you've pretty much drained me," he replied.

"I don't need your cum this time, just a stiff cock," Alice replied. She stood up and pulled her dress up and over her head, handing it to Olivia.

Alice was completely nude under the dress, and Olivia whistled softly in appreciation of her figure. Alice did a spin to show off as Olivia put the dress over a coat hook. Then Alice turned to face the toilet and planted her feet wide, bent over at the waist.

"Fuck me hard, Alex. Please. I need to come so badly," Alice begged.

Olivia practically grabbed his cock and rammed it in her dripping pussy. Alex didn't need any encouragement, and Alice wondered if it was just his fitness regimen or if he'd taken some kind of enhancement in the hopes of having a fantastic evening. Either way, his cock was wonderfully hard inside her, and she was soaking wet before they started.

Alice reached back and put her fingertips to her aching clit, stroking furiously as Alex thrust into her. "Harder, Alex," Olivia urged, "she can take it, can't you, Alice?"

"Fuck yes, fuck me hard, Alex. As hard and fast as you can," Alice agreed.

Alex didn't reply, he just put all his effort into doing as he was asked. To his credit, he lasted long enough for Alice's orgasm to kick into full swing, before he too began to come. When they were done, and the gasping over, Olivia wasted no time in spinning Alice around and sitting her down again, then presenting Alex's dripping cock to her.

Olivia took hold of the back of Alice's head and encourage the two of them to meet. Alice pretended to a little reluctance to play along, until Olivia swore and said, "Suck him clean you dirty little bitch. You know you want it."

With that encouragement, Alice did as she was told, cleaning Alex's cock from the root to the shaft of their combined cum. Olivia's face burned with desire as she watched and Alice knew she was going to be having lots more fun with her, very soon. It seemed inevitable after Olivia had given her her first lesbian kiss.

When they'd washed up, they nonchalantly walked back into the bar, and no-one acknowledged they'd been gone or that anything might have happened. Olivia handed out some mints, and they got more drinks.

There was a great deal of socialising to go that evening, and Alice knew she'd never be able to remember everyone's names but Olivia assured her she had a strategy to cope with that problem, involving computerised flashcards that matched faces to names. Alice giggled at how seriously Olivia took it all but stopped when she was fixed with that imperiously icy glare of hers.

Alex made his excuses after a while, seeing that they wanted to spend some time alone with each other and they chatted for a good hour before finally leaving.

"I hope I'll see you on Saturday, Alice," Olivia said.

"Saturday?"

"At the munch, you are coming, I hope?"

"Oh, are you in the KinkSoc too?"

"I certainly am, so I'll see you there?"

Alice nodded enthusiastically. "I wouldn't miss it for the world."

"That's if I don't see you at the start of Fresher's photoshoot on Thursday. Be there, or be without an awesome photo for your profiles!" Olivia called over her shoulder as she walked down the street.

Alice waved goodbye as her new friend walked off, singing to herself and indeed, everyone within earshot. She pulled out her phone and took a quick look at the photos. They were terrific, and Alice wondered just how much time Olivia spent at the photography club and in what capacity. The evening had been fabulous, but she was already horny again, just flicking through the pictures and she was sure she would make use of Francesca's little bag of goodies the moment she got under her duvet.

Then she added some reminders to her phone about the photo-shoot and other things and headed for the taxi rank.

She was looking forward to the munch, and though the thought of it made her nervous, the photoshoot was bound to be fun if Olivia wanted her there. But before that would happen, she had something else to take care of.

Alice pulled a business card from her purse and looked it over as she waited for the next taxi to pull up.

Perfect, she thought, punching the URL into her phone. Francesca's shop came up quickly.

Tomorrow thought Angela, I'm going shopping.

AUTHOR'S NOTE

Thank you for reading Taught by a Swinger, Book One of the Sexy Student Lessons series. This was first published under the title 'Alternative Freshers' Fair' and the series was going to be 'Freshers' Week'. I liked that, but needed something a little clearer for erotica shorts as it didn't resonate with the audience.

The topic and content remains the same.

A note on terminology for those not familiar with U.K. universities. Freshers' Week is a week of debauchery and nonsense that occurs just before the start of the first semester, for first year students.

As the drinking age in the U.K. is 18, there's a lot of alcohol flowing and young people explore their freedom. This is probably similar to U.S. universities and of course, the real purpose is to get students used to the city, let them join the fencing club or the LARP society, and get themselves square away for their first time living on their own.

Many students in the U.K. spend their first year in halls of residence (dorms). It's not normal for us to share a room with someone though. That two single bed and awkwardness thing that's seen in American films is just downright weird to us!

On the downside, we don't have many campus universities so

you're often rushing from building to building to attend lectures. On the upside, we don't get arrested for drinking because we're old enough at 18, just for stealing traffic cones and drunk and disorderly. :)

Another difference that you might notice is that we call university, university or uni, not college in the U.K. We do have colleges but those are pretty much for 16-18 year olds, you only really find colleges at ancient unis like Oxford and Cambridge (and possibly a few others, I'm not fact checking that for you).

꩜

If you enjoyed the book and can spare the time to leave a review on Amazon or Goodreads, I would greatly appreciate it.

The Sexy Student Lessons series will take place over one hot week of thoroughly wicked play for Alice and the new friends she met at the fair. Can you work out who she's going to play with?

If the series is popular, I'll write more than the initial planned seven books. But that's the outline for now.

Thanks for your support, and for buying the book or borrowing it through Kindle Unlimited.

Your steamily,

K.F. Jones

Submissive Lesbian Personal Assistant

This is a new series about Amber, a young woman who is seduced by her new employer, a dominant and wealthy lesbian.

Punished by Her Lesbian Boss

Seduced by Her Lesbian Boss

ABOUT THE AUTHOR

K.F. Jones is writing in two main worlds. The first is about a young man who finds love in the arms of an older werewolf with a kinky streak. The Consort of the Werewolf King features some very naughty werewolves, that no amount of discipline will tame.

The second is all about strong, confident young women capable of taking on any challenge, in a sexy steampunk world. You'll meet Dawn first, and follow her as she tries to make up for a mistake made while she indulged her passions.

Later you'll meet Mercy, who should be studying at the Academy and concentrating on her exams. If she could just avoid regular disciplinary sessions in the Deputy Head's office, or find a way to keep the demanding Headmistress satiated, perhaps she could finally unravel the conspiracy she's discovered!

If you'd like to find out when new books are released, join the mailing list at the website. **http://kfjones.net/**

f facebook.com/KFJonesbooks

℗ pinterest.com/kfjonesauthor

g goodreads.com/kfjones

a amazon.com/author/kfjonesbooks

🐦 twitter.com/kfjonesauthor

Made in the USA
Middletown, DE
09 September 2022